Best Little Wingman

by Janet Allen

Illustrated by Jim Postier

Boyds Mills Press

Published by Boyds Mills Press, Inc.
A Highlights Company
815 Church Street
Honesdale, Pennsylvania 18431
Printed in China

Publisher Cataloging-in-Publication Data   (U.S.)

Allen, Janet.
Best little wingman / by Janet Allen ; illustrated by Jim Postier.—1st ed.
[32] p. : col. ill. ; cm.
ISBN 1-59078-197-X
1. Fathers and daughters—Fiction—Juvenile literature. 2. Snowplows—Fiction—Juvenile literature. 3. Night—Fiction—Juvenile literature. I. Postier, Jim. II. Title.
[E] 21   PZ7.J55Bl 2005

First edition, 2005
The text is set in 14-point Wilke Roman.
The illustrations are done in watercolor.

Visit our Web site at www.boydsmillspress.com

10 9 8 7 6 5 4 3 2 1

With love and gratitude for my father, Murle Bean,
who taught me how to be the best wingman I could be
— J. A.

For Beth Ann and the children, with special thanks
to the Brogan family
— J. P.

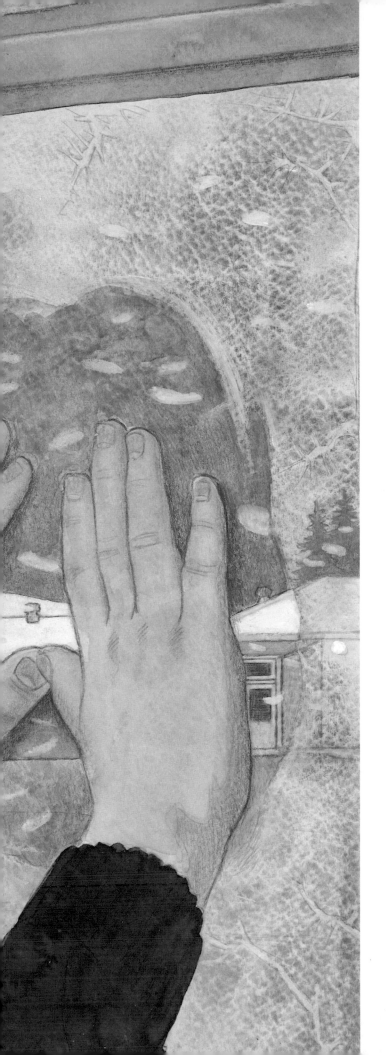

JANNY PRESSED HER FINGERS against the icy kitchen window, watching for headlights on the road. She knew that when her fingers melted all the ice, her father would come to take her for a ride in the big snowplow.

"Come away from that window and eat your supper," her mother called as she pulled a pan of hot biscuits from the oven. Janny was tempted by the sweet smell. But she couldn't leave her window.

"I'd be surprised if your father took you with him tonight," her mother said. "It's too cold, and it's snowing too hard. He'll be plowing the roads all night."

Janny knew her mother was wrong. Her father would take her out tonight because he needed her help. It was her job to pull the lever that raised the plow's right wing, so the big plow didn't knock over people's mailboxes along the road.

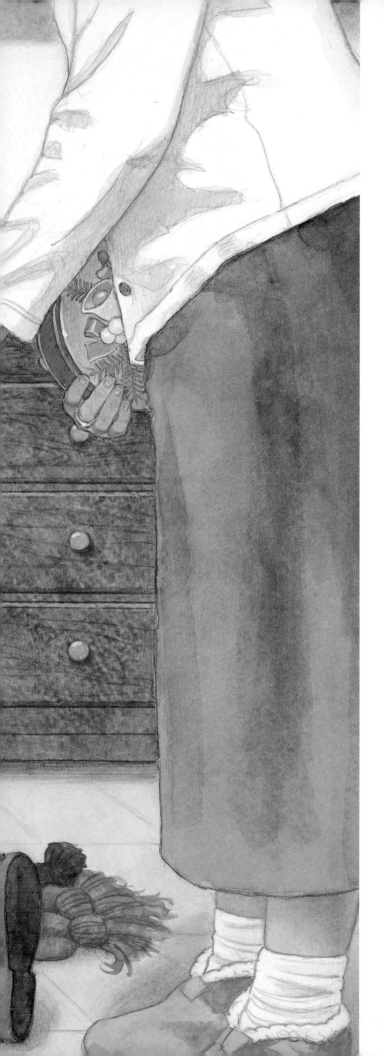

Suddenly, she heard the snowplow's blade as it scraped the road. She saw the truck's lights shine through the snowy night. Janny ran to the door, just as the plow stopped at the end of the driveway.

"Is my wingman ready to go?" her dad asked from the doorway.

Janny looked toward her mother.

"Better bundle up tight," her mother told her.

Janny hurried to put on her jacket, hat, scarf, and mittens.

Her mother filled a tin with warm biscuits. She poured hot chocolate into a Thermos. "Don't stay out too late," she warned Janny as she handed her the treats. Then Janny and her father headed into the snowy night.

Her dad lifted her up so she could put her foot on the metal step near the door. Then, she grabbed the handles and pulled herself into the cab. Her dad jumped into the truck, lowered the V-shaped plow, and continued plowing the Egypt Road.

Janny watched carefully so she could see the mailboxes before they got too close. She pulled the lever to lift the wing as they approached each mailbox. Then she pushed the lever to make the wing go back down after they passed each house. "Good job," her dad said. "What kind of plowmen would we be if people couldn't get their mail tomorrow?"

They made a sweep around the post office and plowed the road in front of Tuft's General Store. At the Baptist church, they turned and headed up the hill. Janny could see Dr. Turner, the veterinarian, waving as they neared his driveway.

"Is the Tompkins Road blocked?" he asked her dad. "I need to head out there and look after a sick horse. Say, Beanie, who's that in the truck with you?"

"My best wingman is with me tonight."

Janny waved to Dr. Turner.

"Follow me, Doc," her dad said. "We'll head out to the Tompkins Road and see what there is to see."

When they reached the Tompkins Road, they found it blocked with drifting snow. The big plow pushed slowly through the snow like a great elephant. Dr. Turner honked his horn in thanks and headed for the farm with the sick horse.

They drove past the Smiths' house, where the barn looked like a mountain of snow. They plowed by the Kennedys', snow flying from both sides of the plow as it picked up speed.

Janny could rest now. There were no more houses and no more mailboxes for miles.

"Better head out to the Young Lake Road now," her dad said. "How about some of those biscuits and hot chocolate?"

Janny handed one of the warm biscuits to her father and poured two cups of hot chocolate.

"Don't spill that now," said her dad.

Suddenly, they saw a light up ahead. A car was stuck in a snowbank. A man was waving his arms. "Looks like Mr. Watson," said Janny.

Her dad stopped the plow and leaned in front of Janny so he could roll down the window. "Hey, Ollie! What are you doing driving in those snowdrifts?"

"Couldn't see a thing, Beanie. Lucky for me those drifts were there, or I would have been in the brook," Mr. Watson shouted.

Janny watched her dad jump from the cab and hook a heavy chain to Mr. Watson's bumper. Mr. Watson got back behind the steering wheel of his car as her dad climbed back into the truck. He put the truck in reverse and slowly pulled the car out of the snow.

When the car was safely on the road, her dad stopped and jumped out of the cab. He unhooked the chain and threw it into the back of the truck. "That should do it. Now keep that car between the snowdrifts, Ollie!"

Janny was getting tired. She was
tired from a night of seeing what she
could see, but she knew there was
one more stop. The lights from the
Wilson house soon peeked through
the blowing snow. Her dad turned
into the Wilsons' driveway, pushing
the snow to the side of the garage.

Mrs. Wilson waved them down
from the front step. Janny climbed
over to her father's side of the truck
as Mrs. Wilson trudged through the
snow carrying a package. Janny could
smell the warm molasses cookies
with maple frosting even before her
father handed them to her. "Thank
you, Mrs. Wilson, for the nice
surprise," her dad said.

"Thank you," said Janny.

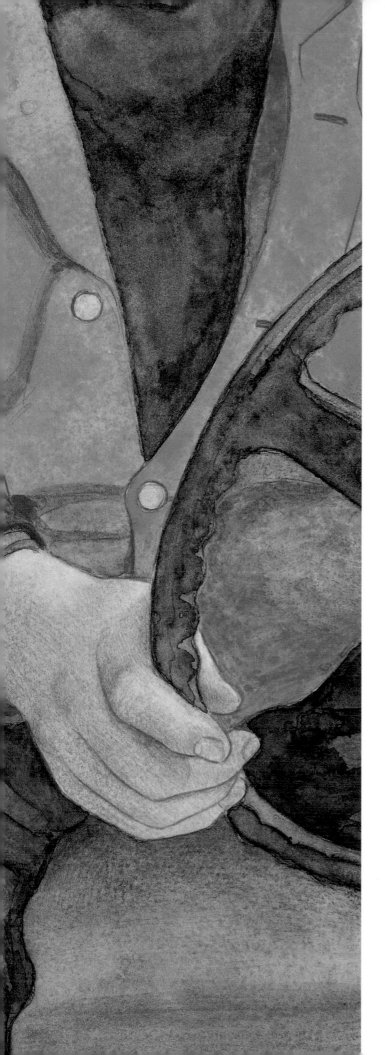

Janny and her dad began the long drive back.

"Are we finished for the night?" she asked. The warm cab was making her feel sleepy, but she didn't want to fall asleep yet. She didn't want her dad to think she was too little to do her job.

"The roads look good here, so I think I'll drop you off and then swing across the Wambolt Road just to make sure Mr. Wambolt can get in his driveway when he gets home from work tonight."

Janny soon fell asleep to the rhythm of the wheels on the road.

When she opened her eyes, she could feel the wet snow on her face. Her father carried her up the driveway and through the kitchen door, where her mother stood waiting.

As her mother and father helped her out of her snowsuit and into bed, Janny's dad whispered to her, "You did a good night's work, little wingman. I couldn't have done my work without you."

Then he headed back out into the cold night.

Many snowy nights would come and go before her dad's work was finally done. The little girl became a woman who spent her days seeing what there was to see in many wonderful places. But as she pressed her fingers against the icy kitchen window, she only wished she could see the lights from her dad's snowplow just one more time. The snow blurred her vision, and for just one moment she thought she could hear her dad whisper, "You did a good night's work, little wingman."